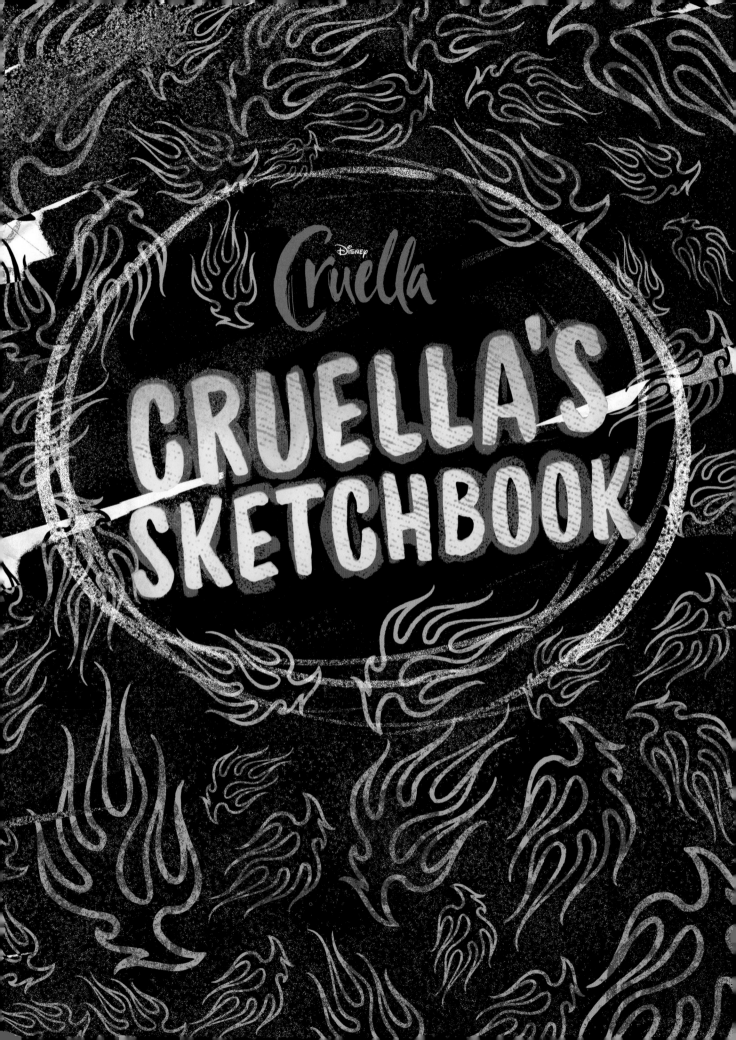

Disney Cruella

CRUELLA'S SKETCHBOOK

Adapted by Tina McCleef
Screenplay by Dana Fox and Tony McNamara
Story by Aline Brosh McKenna and Kelly Marcel & Steve Zissis
Based upon the novel "The One Hundred and One Dalmatians"
by Dodie Smith

Printed in the United States of America
First Hardcover Edition, April 2021
1 3 5 7 9 10 8 6 4 2
FAC-034274-21057
Library of Congress Control Number: 2020943494
ISBN 978-1-368-06233-6

Design by Soyoung Kim

Visit disneybooks.com

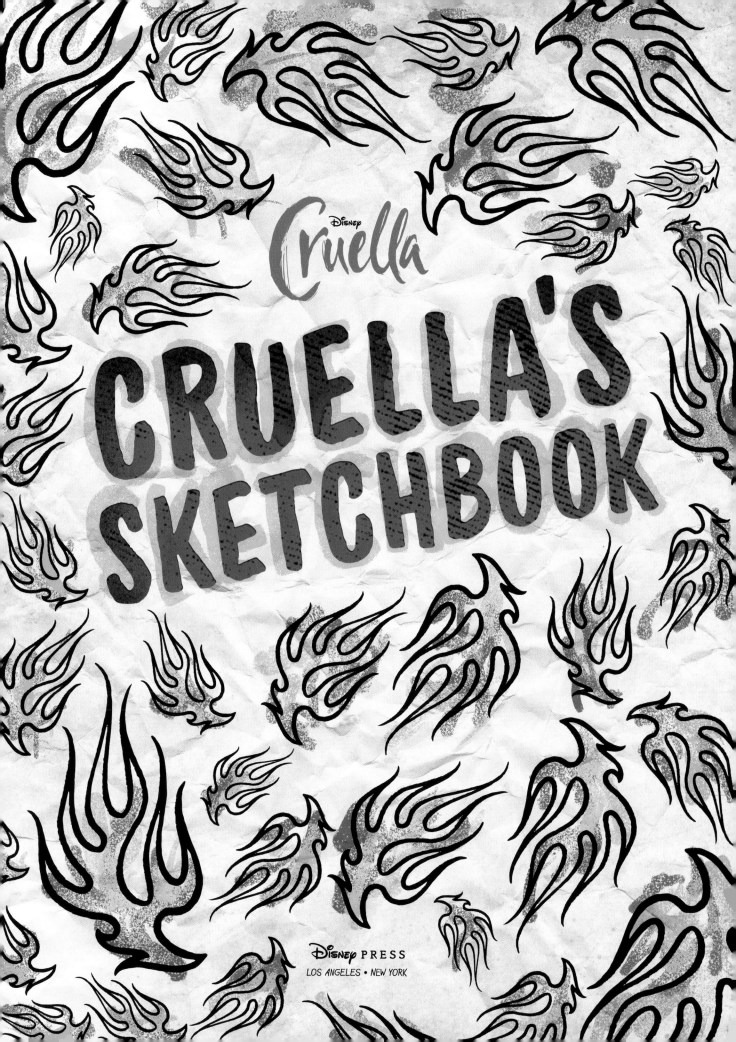

Disney
Cruella

CRUELLA'S SKETCHBOOK

DISNEY PRESS
LOS ANGELES • NEW YORK

If you have found this sketchbook, it means I, Estella, have either risen to stardom in the fashion world or faded into obscurity. My mates Horace and Jasper got me this book as a sort of early birthday present. They said now I have one place to put all my designs. A place to keep them forever. At first I wasn't sure if I'd really use it . . . I normally tape my sketches on the wall of our flat so I can see how different looks work together, almost like I'm piecing together my very own fashion line. But then I found some of the old drawings from when Horace, Jasper, and I first took our pickpocket operation to the next level. I also have so many brilliant designs from growing up, too, and my time in the cottage with Mum. I couldn't let them just sit under the bed, collecting dust. . . .

So I present to you, reader who should not be reading this (seriously, what are you doing with my book?) . . .

THE LIFE AND WORK OF ESTELLA

FAMous
My rules

ME

AKA

my
SKETCHBOOK

OUCH

The world has never understood my greatness, even when I was a little girl. When other children were out playing in the garden, I was digging through my mum's pile of fabric scraps, pulling together my own designs. I'd rip up the patterns she had and create ones that were all my own. After all, everyone knows that great artists don't just break the rules—THEY COMPLETELY REINVENT THEM.

MUM

My mum was one of those really "good" people, the kind who helped little old ladies cross the street and brought chicken soup to sick neighbors. She was a washerwoman, mending and ironing until her fingers were cracked and pink. She did it all so we could eat and keep a nice little flat. It might've been small, but it was cozy. I have so many happy memories there.

When I turned five, she bought me this special tea set, with little saucers and cream and sugar and everything. We climbed into a tree and had our tea up there, just because I thought it would be more fun.

oh darling

HOMe

"You're one of a kind," Mum said, and she smiled at me like I was the most special little girl in all of England. "Happy birthday."

When I turned twelve, Mum said I must go to a fine country day school and get a proper education. The only problems were the POLYESTER UNIFORMS and the fact that all the kids knew I was there on scholarship. I couldn't control the other students, but I decided I wasn't going to walk through the halls like another boring, unimaginative git, destined to be behind some trading desk. I was an artist, a rebel heart. I didn't fit in there and I didn't want to.

FIRST DAY OF SCHOOL

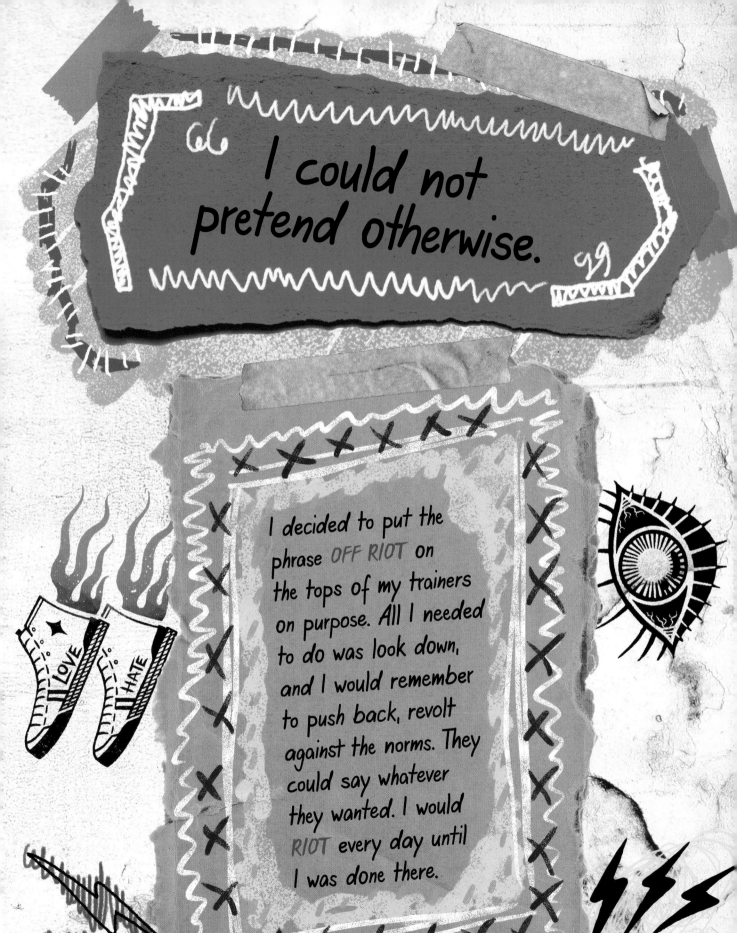

I could not pretend otherwise.

I decided to put the phrase OFF RIOT on the tops of my trainers on purpose. All I needed to do was look down, and I would remember to push back, revolt against the norms. They could say whatever they wanted. I would RIOT every day until I was done there.

My first few weeks at my new school didn't go quite as well as planned. I promised Mum I wouldn't completely lose my temper. When I'd get so *angry* I wanted to scream, Mum would say that was "*cruella*," my alter ego. She told me to control my temper. She wanted me to think about forgiveness, and how I could be a better person, and all that nonsense. She thought if I could just get Cruella under control, her dear, sweet Estella would shine through.

Mean Ginger

SIMPLY SOUR

So when Cruella reared her wicked head, I'd just say, "Thanks for coming, but you may go now." I kept repeating that to myself when I met the mean ginger and his little friend. I kept repeating it when he said I looked like a skunk, and then when he threw a massive spitball at my face. I was still repeating it when I dragged him into the yard and beat the pulp out of him.

Annoying Lackey

Run the World

ICON

I really tried to be good and do what Mum said. There was one girl—Anita—who was always kind to me, and when I felt miffed, I tried to remind myself there were still some decent people out there. But Mean Ginger and his friend made my life so hard. It seemed like everywhere I went, there they were. I couldn't get in trouble again for some prank they blamed me for, and I absolutely could not listen to the headmaster call me a charity case one more time. IT WAS NOT FAIR.

Not REAL

CRUELLA VS ESTELLA

CRUELLA
- guarded
- thinks about revenge
- no manners
- can't control her temper

ESTELLA
- polite
- thinks about forgiveness
- kind
- controls her temper

One day I was eating lunch, minding my own business, when Mean Ginger and all his mates grabbed me. They lifted me up and tossed me right into a rubbish bin behind school. I was Cruella then. Every part of me wanted to RAGE and SCREAM and FIGHT, even if I got expelled. I didn't care who saw or who heard me—I JUST WANTED REVENGE.

School of Nasty

BIG BULLY.

Only one good thing came out of it: I found a tiny puppy in the dumpster, beneath some old takeaway containers. I wasn't going to leave some poor helpless creature in the rubbish bin. I named the little guy BUDDY, and that's what he's become to me. Sometimes it felt like he was my only friend. He was the one who curled up by my feet when I was up late, working on my designs. He loved to run circles around me in the garden or play tug-of-war with some old fabric scraps. Buddy was so brilliant he almost made me forget how awful Mean Ginger and his mates were. ALMOST.

ADORE ME

ME & BUDDY

Mum kept telling me to let Mean Ginger's bullying go, to turn the other cheek. But how many cheeks can one person have? I was so tired of being pushed around. I needed to let Mean Ginger know I wasn't going to take whatever nastiness he delivered. I wanted him to know I wasn't afraid.

I came up with the most DELICIOUS PRANK. I set bottles of green dye in every single locker and rigged a device that sprayed it as soon as someone opened the door. Oh, it was so satisfying seeing the look on Mean Ginger's smug little face. He was spitting out the green dye and wiping it from his eyes. I was quite enjoying it when the headmaster yanked me away.

He called my mum in, and she and the headmaster had it out. The headmaster kept trying to expel me, but my mum said she was withdrawing me from the school. They went back and forth like that for a while—"I'm expelling her!" "I already withdrew her!" Then Mum really let him have it. "Your school turns out horrible children with no creativity or compassion," she snapped. She was livid. She couldn't believe he'd treat me that way. She couldn't understand why they didn't see how TALENTED and SPECIAL I was.

It turned out that one prank cost us a lot. Those little twerps told their parents about it, and my mum's business slowed. No one wanted to take their laundry to the mother of such a vile creature. Mum was brilliant, though, and never let it get her down. She decided this was just the chance we needed. We'd make a go of it in London. It would be a new start, a chance to pursue my dreams of being a fashion designer. Mum promised me that as soon as we got there, we'd find REGENT'S PARK and have tea by the fountain.

GLORY RIOT

We packed up our clunky little car and were on our way. Mum just wanted to make one stop first: some place called Hellman Hall. The giant stone mansion had high walls and a turret, like it belonged in the pages of some fairy tale. Lightning streaked the sky. Mum told me to lie low and stay in the car while she talked to someone inside.

Mum's Necklace

shiny gold chain

red jewel in the center

She gave me her special necklace to hold on to before she took off across the drive. I just stared at it for a moment, unable to believe it was in my hands. I'd never seen anything so beautiful before. It had these ornate gold details on it, and a giant red jewel in the center that always sat flat against Mum's neck. It was her prized possession—one of the most valuable things she owned.

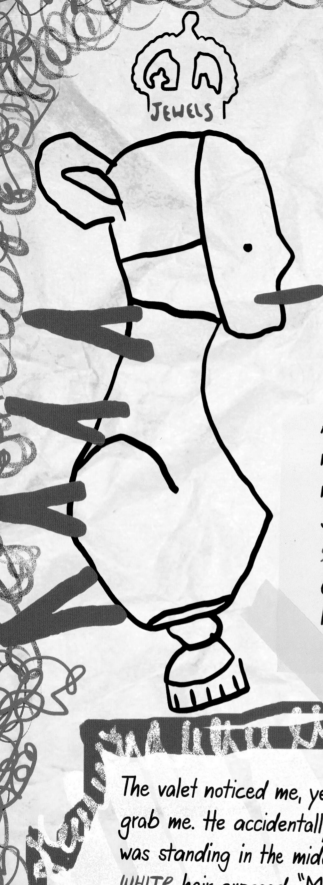

JEWELS

I sat in the car, holding that necklace. I was trying to be good, but then I saw all these posh women in floor-length ball gowns going up the front stairs. They were in chiffon and fur, tulle and silks. I had to go inside and see the party for myself. Buddy and I snuck in through a kitchen door and hitched a ride on a server's food cart.

As I looked at all the people in their magnificent gowns and ensembles, I did my best to stay out of trouble. But then Buddy saw this cape that was made of SQUIrrel Furs, and that was the beginning of the end. He bolted from the cart, and I chased him through the ballroom.

The valet noticed me, yelled for me to stop, and tried to grab me. He accidentally pulled off my hat, and suddenly I was standing in the middle of the ballroom, my BLaCK-anD-WHITe hair exposed. "My god," he said in disgust. "Put that hat on before somebody sees."

Who did he think he was, THE HAIR POLICE?

That was when ol' cruella came out to play. Here he was, this stranger, telling me I should hide my hair—my TRUE SELF. I couldn't help wanting some sweet revenge. I spotted a massive cake. I turned and knocked it over, sending it into the runway models and the rest of the crowd.

THE MYSTERIOUS MARIE ANTOINETTE

The valet looked like his head might rocket off his body. He was FURIOUS. I knew that was our chance, though: it had given us the perfect distraction to get away. I darted up the staircase with Buddy and we made it out a side door.

Even now, I can still remember this amazing dress a woman at the party wore. I've sketched it here. She looked like Marie Antoinette.

That was when I saw Mum. She was standing on the cliff's edge, talking to some woman. They were far away, and I couldn't make out the woman's face or what she was wearing. I ran toward them. The grounds were dark. Suddenly, THREE LARGE DALMATIANS bounded out of the house and chased after Buddy and me. When I called out for Mum, she couldn't hear me over the crashing of the waves below. The dogs kept on us, and we tumbled down a hill and landed in a hedge.

No

Suddenly, there was this horrible HIGH-PITCHED SOUND, and the Dalmatians jumped over the hedge and raced across the lawn. They charged Mum. She lost her balance and fell backward into the ocean below.

I was frozen, staring out at the cliff where Mum had been standing just a few seconds before. At some point the police came. "I had no idea my dogs were on the loose," the woman said. "I think they were chasing someone." The police started searching the grounds for me. We had to leave, we had to run, or I would've been taken to some dreadful orphanage somewhere. Buddy and I jumped into a passing lorry, and I fell into the bed of the vehicle, hitting my head. The last thing I remember was Buddy licking my face. Then everything went dark.

When I finally woke up, we were in LONDON. It all felt like an awful nightmare I'd had. I'd lost Mum's necklace at some point, and that seemed like the only proof it had even happened. IT COULDN'T BE real; I didn't want it to be. Mum couldn't really be gone.

When the lorry passed Regent's Park, Buddy and I jumped down, and we found the fountain Mum had promised we'd have tea at. It was COLD and DARK. The park was completely empty. Even with Buddy there, I'd never felt more alone in my entire life. It was all my fault; I never should've gone inside. If I'd just stayed in the car and done as Mum told me to do, none of this would've happened. If I hadn't let my temper get the better of me and I hadn't knocked over that stupid cake, those wretched Dalmatians wouldn't have come after us. They wouldn't have charged Mum. We would all be together still, our small but happy family.

Buddy licked away my tears. I pulled him close as I curled up on a park bench. I didn't know where to go or what to do. The world seemed so BIG and FRIGHTENING without Mum to guide me through it. I kept trying to tell myself it would be okay, but nothing was okay anymore. I was an orphan, with nothing and no one.

That night was the first time I'd ever CRIED myself to sleep.

The next morning, I noticed two boys in the park running scams. They had a little Chihuahua named Wink, who wore an eye patch. They'd work together, using distractions to steal wallets. Eventually they spotted me lying on a bench. Jasper, the taller one, said he wanted to help me, but his mate, Horace, wasn't convinced.

They might've stood there, arguing back and forth about whether I should join their gang, but the constable came looking for them. We all bolted down an alley, trying to get away. I followed Horace and Jasper through a hole in a brick building, then up an abandoned staircase. We ended up in some kind of secret lair.

Even when we were safe in their hideout, Horace still didn't think I should stay. "Where are your parents?" he asked in this annoyed voice.

It was a while before I managed to tell them that my mum had died and I had nowhere to go. Horace was still being a twit, but Jasper was kind. "I'm thinking you should stay here, be part of our gang," he said. "We could use a girl to look innocent and be a distraction." I know I should have jumped at the chance; it meant a place to live, a way to get food and everything I needed. But I wanted to be a fashion designer, not some petty criminal.

I was starting to realize it didn't matter what I wanted. I didn't have choices anymore. All my dreams DIED the night Mum fell off that cliff. I had lost my mum, my only family. I'D LOST EVERYTHING.

That was the day I agreed to be part of Horace and Jasper's gang. I knew one thing was going to have to change, though. Horace dug through old boxes and found some dye. I grabbed a bottle of the red one and went to work over the busted sink. It wasn't that I didn't like my hair. I've always thought it was what made me different . . . special. But I thought about the valet's face when he had yanked off my cap. He'd scrunched his nose, like he was disgusted with me. That was when I'd lost my temper. How many times had Mum told me not to be so cross?

It's really not worth thinking too much about. What's done is done. Besides, a shock of black-and-white hair was too distinctive for a thief. I wanted to blend in with the rest of London. I wanted to move, unnoticed, through the crowds.

STAY WEIRD

I dumped the whole bottle of dye onto my hair, working it down to the roots. I stared at myself in the mirror when I was done. The red made my green eyes pop. It made my pale complexion seem even paler. I scrunched up my nose, making the same face the valet had made when he saw me.

Make Your Mark

WHO'S THE MEAN GINGER NOW?

Jasper and Horace had run the same tired schemes a hundred times before. When I first started working with them, we were always getting chased by the police. Jasper would nick a wallet, then toss it to Wink, who'd take it to Horace. By the time it got to me, half of London was screaming for our arrest. I knew we'd have to be smarter, more cunning, if we wanted to succeed as thieves. I was walking past a tailor shop one day when I had an idea. Horace, Jasper, and I took the pups on a little adventure that night. We went to the tailor shop and slipped Wink through a tiny window in the back. He got the lock open from the inside, and we took a sewing machine and as many bolts of fabric as we could carry. I found some great patterns I knew would be useful. We brought it all home and I went to work.

FASHION·MAKES ART MAKES· ·FASHION

fashion

STOP IT!

E

ICON

There's a difference between being a GOOD THIEF and being a GREAT THIEF. It's the element of surprise.

RUN

Everything changed once I started sewing for Horace and Jasper. I designed every kind of costume I could dream up. Altar boy robes, butler uniforms, prep school uniforms, fancy gowns that would help me pass as a posh socialite, Boy Scout uniforms, and a three-piece suit that made even the boys look dashing. Whenever we had a new scheme, we blended in perfectly.

Everyone just assumed we were exactly where we should be, doing exactly what we should be doing. As I grew older, my stitches got straighter and more even. I knew how to finish seams and hem and sew mitered corners. I could sew elaborate silk linings into jackets and dresses. My darts and pleats were perfect. I wasn't just good at it—I was great.

Once we were old enough to drive, Horace posed as my chauffeur for a speedy getaway while I played the part of a high-society lady to sneak into the richest parts of town.

[POSH WOMAN AND HER DRIVER]

HERE ARE SOME OF MY FAVORITE DESIGNS FOR OUR VARIOUS CONS. AREN'T THEY BRILLIANT?

CLASSIC SUIT

Always versatile, always in style. We've used this outfit a dozen times for different jobs. It is great to pose as a waiter or to blend in at a fancy event.

BUSINESS CHIC

Horace, Jasper, and I used this once on a crowded bus. It was one of my best scams. We got on separately and pretended not to know each other. Jasper and I went through, picking the pockets of several businessmen and then dropping the wallets on the floor. Wink ran them to Horace, depositing each of them into his umbrella. Horace walked off and we all went our separate ways. No one knew a thing.

A good hotel uniform is essential. Jasper, Horace, and I love cleaning up at hotels. Literally. Last time we posed as room service, we stole a watch, a miniature television, and lots of expensive jewelry.

HOTEL STAFF LOOK

Always remember the tools of the trade.

RICH DIVA ENSEMBLE

This required a bit of extra makeup to really tie in the look. Wink also made the perfect accessory. After all, what rich woman doesn't have a small dog on her arm?

House of Baroness
LONDON

I used to see these House of Baroness London ads everywhere. On buses, on billboards, in magazines. Seeing the logo of such a prominent designer all over the city was a constant reminder that what I was currently doing and what I wanted to be doing were two very different things.

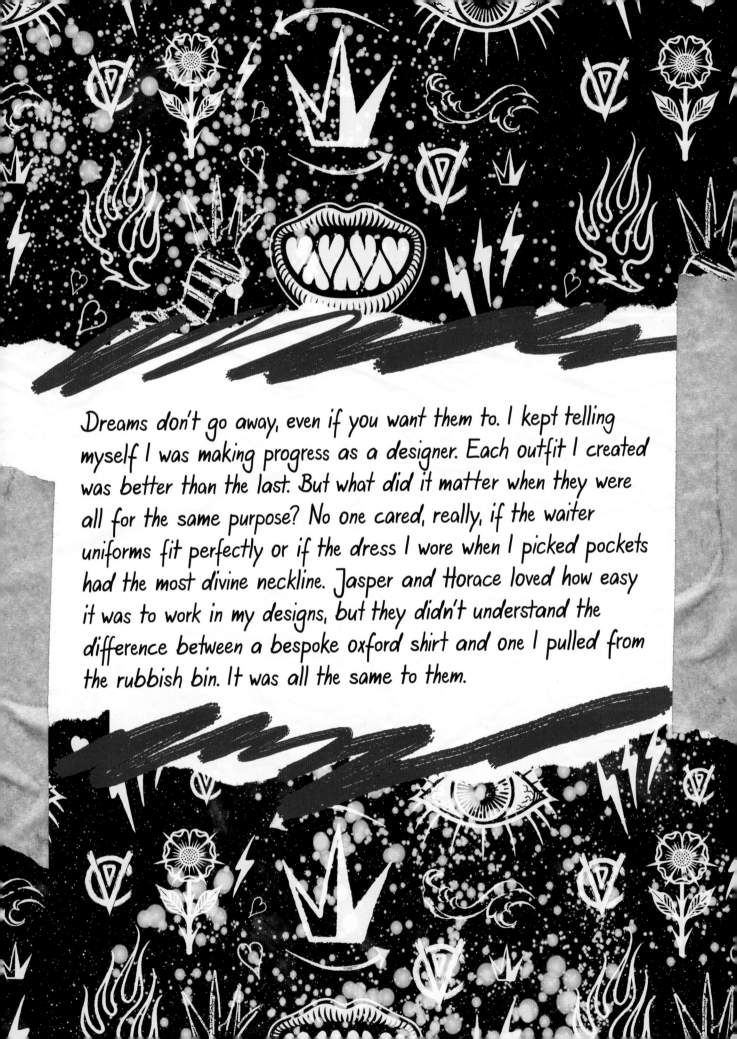

Dreams don't go away, even if you want them to. I kept telling myself I was making progress as a designer. Each outfit I created was better than the last. But what did it matter when they were all for the same purpose? No one cared, really, if the waiter uniforms fit perfectly or if the dress I wore when I picked pockets had the most divine neckline. Jasper and Horace loved how easy it was to work in my designs, but they didn't understand the difference between a bespoke oxford shirt and one I pulled from the rubbish bin. It was all the same to them.

I wanted to know what it was like to be a real designer. To see my creations coming down the runway. To work with delicate fabrics imported from all over the world. I wanted people to take me seriously and give me feedback on what I had done. It was hard to imagine that I might never become a real designer, working at a real company.

I didn't want to give up my dreams, but I couldn't help thinking the world didn't want a designer like me—with no education, no posh university credits. I was really starting to believe that maybe this was all my life would ever be. . . .

ART WILL SURVIVE

And now, here I am, still designing for our schemes. Today is my birthday. Birthdays aren't much of a thing for me, at least not since Mum died. But Jasper and Horace got it in their heads that they would celebrate me this year. In addition to giving me this journal, on the day of my birthday they dressed Buddy and Wink up in tiny party hats and made a cake. Then Jasper delivered the most brilliant news: he'd gotten me a job at LIBERTY OF LONDON.

Liberty is one of the poshest shops in Mayfair. They have elegant coats and bags and their own fabric line. I don't know how Jasper did it (and I don't really want to know), but I'm starting next week. I almost screamed when he told me. This is what I've been waiting for: a REAL CHANCE at my dream. Mum would be so proud.

The sneaky blokes caught my face when they gave me my letter of employment.

I used to think "liberty" meant "FREEDOM." Now whenever I hear the word, I break out in hives.

There's so much opportunity at the shop. There's a whole floor of seamstresses, and there are shopgirls styling outfits and women behind the jewelry counter who could talk about cushion cut diamonds for days. I thought that as soon as my boss, GERALD, discovered how good I was with a sewing machine, he'd promote me to the alterations department. But it's been weeks and I'm still stuck in the basement. I'm mopping floors and emptying rubbish bins and scrubbing the loo. I've tried to do my work with a smile, but my boss makes it IMPOSSIBLE. He's always yelling, "This toilet needs plunging!" or "Why didn't you dust my office?"

When I try to talk to Gerald about my goals, he won't listen to a thing I say. He refuses to give me a chance. He just sees me as another UNEDUCATED TWIT destined to do menial work for the rest of her life.

my Liberty uniform

If only he could see my designs . . .

Yesterday I was sacked, made redundant, fired. Whatever you want to call it. My career at Liberty was officially over. I'd done every single thing Gerald had asked me to. I'd scrubbed the loos and his office and every inch of the hall. I'd gone to the alley behind the shop to throw out some rubbish when the bag broke all over me. I was covered head to toe in coffee grounds, fabric scraps, and banana peels. As if that wasn't enough, I'd locked myself out. I had to walk inside through the front entrance, past all these smartly dressed women, who stared at me like I was a stray dog.

I'm so glad Jasper and Horace caught me during such a fun moment. NOT.

Getting fired doesn't look good on anyone.

Apparently Gerald wasn't pleased with my attitude, because he sacked me on the spot. He told me to clean his office one more time before I left and then give back my uniform. While I was dusting and mopping, I kept thinking that was it; it was really over. I'D BARELY LASTED A MONTH.

By the time I finished cleaning, I was the last one in the shop. I walked past the front window display on my way out, but I couldn't bear to see the display's poor, helpless mannequin in a hideous hat. It was terrible, the way that designer put all those clashing fabrics together. I climbed right into the window and went to work. I took a black marker to the plain white wall behind her, and soon I was sketching different friends she might have, people to witness her style and grace. Then I rearranged the fabric to create this GORGEOUS overflowing skirt. I kept going, adding on more fabric until it made sense to me. I added a chair that she was kicking over, and I took out my red lipstick, because the whole scene needed REAL COLOR. Something to make it POP. I don't know how long I was there, but at some point I must've fallen asleep.

Gerald found me the next morning. It didn't matter that half of London had gathered outside the window to admire my work. No, Gerald was huffing and yelling and saying he'd call the police on me for what I'd done. I might've been arrested had she not chosen that exact moment to visit the shop.

I'll never forget the first time I saw her:
Baroness von Hellman, the creator of the fashion
label House of Baroness. She was exactly as
I'd imagined—all style and grace. Her dark hair
was pinned in an updo, each strand perfectly
in place. Every accessory and piece of jewelry
worked with her outfit. I'd rehearsed what I'd
say to her a hundred times before, when I was
picking over rooms in the hotel or passing one of
her billboards. But right then I was completely
speechless.

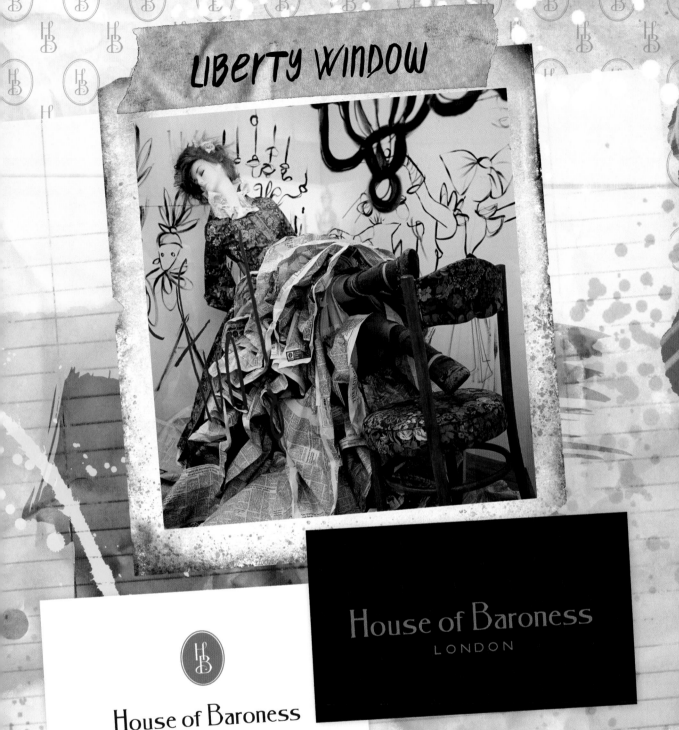

LIBERTY WINDOW

House of Baroness
LONDON

House of Baroness
LONDON

The Baroness was flanked on either side by assistants and bodyguards. You can imagine how stunned I was when she immediately asked who redesigned the front window. Her assistant handed me her card and told me I was hired. "That girl has put together the best window display that I've seen you do in ten years," the Baroness said to Gerald.

BARONESS'S STYLE

* not a hair out of place
* classic accessories
* dress tailored to perfection

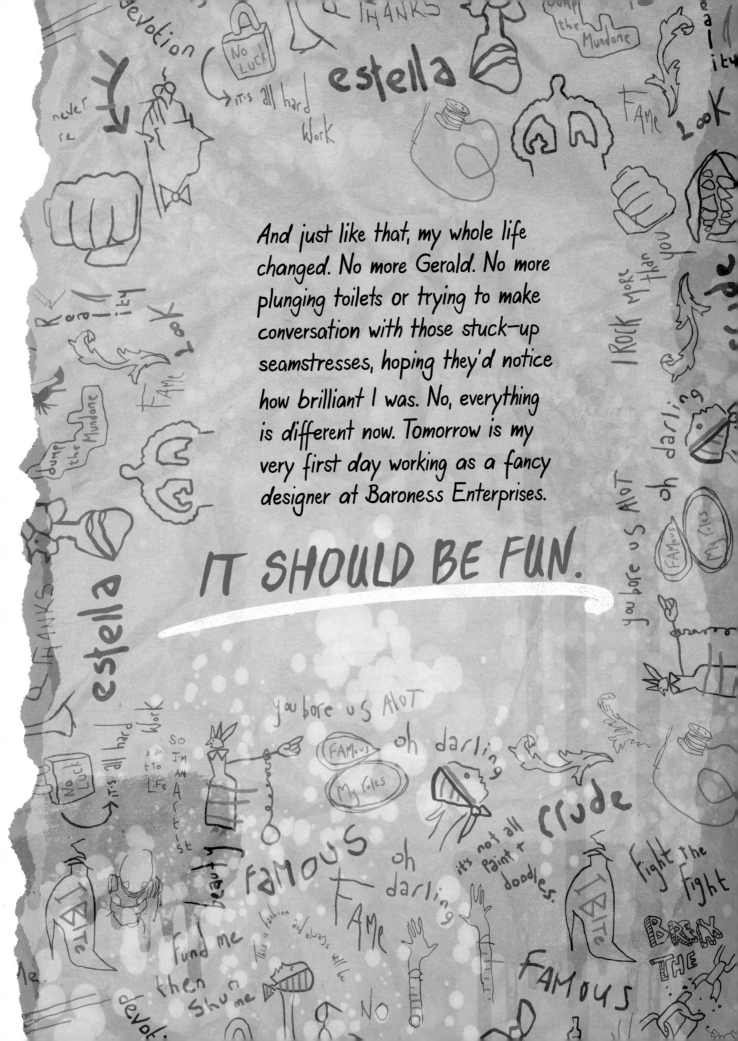

And just like that, my whole life changed. No more Gerald. No more plunging toilets or trying to make conversation with those stuck-up seamstresses, hoping they'd notice how brilliant I was. No, everything is different now. Tomorrow is my very first day working as a fancy designer at Baroness Enterprises.

IT SHOULD BE FUN.

THE TATTLETALE

AUDIENCE MARVELS AT THE BARONESS'S LATEST RUNWAY SHOW

BY ANITA DARLING

The latest runway show by the Baroness was a huge success, with celebrities and designers traveling from all over Europe to get a glimpse of her newest collection. The Baroness stunned with her reinvention of the A-line. She works with a bias cut and a higher line that reshapes the silhouette in such an audacious way the audience broke into rapturous applause at first sight. This latest show secures her place in the fashion world as one of the most heralded designers of our time. She really is a genius. A triumph.

I was so excited when I walked into BARONESS ENTERPRISES for the first time. The lobby of the warehouse was lined with mannequins wearing the most beautiful gowns I'd ever seen. A spotlight shone down on each one, like they were splendid jewels. I pushed through the double doors and into the main design floor. I'd never felt more alive. Dozens of designers were hunched over their sketch pads, creating, and a dozen more gathered fabric over mannequins. A whole line of models waited to try on whatever had been sewn the previous day. The Baroness had the richest, lushest materials I'd ever seen. Bolts and bolts of fabric in every color and texture.

FIRST DAY LOOK

THE BARONESS AT WORK

The Baroness immediately put me to work on her NEW COLLECTION. She wanted as many looks as we designers could pull together. I sketched furiously, inspired by a bolt of pink fabric I'd seen. I wanted it to feel like I was playing with the feminine pink ideal and making it something edgier—BOLDER.

The Baroness sacked three designers before she even saw what I'd made. She studied it, then pulled out this little razor blade. With just a few quick slashes, she removed some excess fabric and trimmed the silhouette. "Hmmmmm. Not bad," she finally said.

From the Baroness?
THAT'S A HUGE COMPLIMENT!
House of Baroness
LONDON
ouse of Baroness
LONDON

House of Bar[...]
LONDON

✿ prim and proper
✿ elegant ladies
ready for their
afternoon tea

My first few weeks with the Baroness have been a whirlwind. She is a tough woman to please and has her team constantly making new designs. The other day I walked into the Baroness's office and two men were sitting in front of her, their shoulders stooped. I suppose they were the heads of department stores that stocked her line. They must've tried to tell the Baroness what to do, because she was livid. She yelled at them and threw them out, furious that they'd try to give her advice.

The Baroness is the MOST POWERFUL person I've ever met. She might not be the nicest boss, and she doesn't apologize, but she doesn't hem and haw when she's making decisions. She just knows exactly what she wants every minute of every day. IT's a revelation.

Today I went with the Baroness to IPSWICH manor, her primary city residence. The place is magnificent. Every piece of furniture is covered in lush velvet, and she has a whole room filled with jewels. Watching how her staff flocks to her side, tugging at her dress and fixing her hem . . . I couldn't help being a little jealous. One day I'll be the boss, the lady of my own manor. I'll be the one ordering people around, instead of the one taking the orders.

House of Baroness
LONDON

❀Hats are for confident people
❀Dresses must have the neatest of pleats

My head's SPINNING. I keep taking these long, deep breaths, trying to calm down, but it isn't working. Today I was helping the Baroness with a design she was working on, and when I turned around, I noticed this brilliant RED PENDANT around her neck. I recognized it immediately. It was the same necklace Mum had—the one she'd given me the night she'd died. A knot rose in the back of my throat.

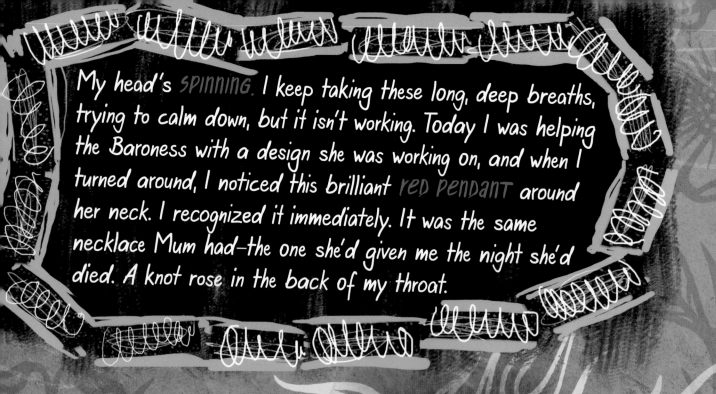

When I pointed to it, the Baroness said the necklace was a family heirloom and some employee had STOLEN it from her years before. That was when it hit me. The woman my mother had been talking to the night she died by the cliff had been THE BARONESS!

HARD AT WORK

The Baroness went into this whole story about how Mum was trying to shake her down for money, then fell off a cliff. "It was during my winter ball, and her death really overshadowed the whole thing," she said in this horribly callous way. She didn't care that Mum had died. She just kept on about how annoyed she was that Mum had asked for money to help her kid.

I probably shouldn't have said anything. I should have known better. But I couldn't help it: I needed to defend Mum. "Maybe she just loved her kid," I finally said, but the Baroness was quick to snap back, "Maybe she had only one person to take care of and she failed dismally." Then she picked up two cucumber slices and put them over her eyes. Apparently it was time for her nap.

I was left stunned. How dare the Baroness speak about Mum like she was so beneath her that her death didn't matter! How dare she say Mum was some scam artist, a crook! How dare she say she was a bad mother!

I've tried to let the Baroness's words go, to pretend like it didn't happen. I've tried to stuff down all my bad feelings and not let them get the better of me. But I can't, not when it comes to my mum. The Baroness is having a gala in the coming weeks. She's been planning it for ages. I'm going to use it as an opportunity to sneak in and take back Mum's necklace, along with all the other jewels in the Baroness's safe. I'll make the Black and White Ball one she'll never forget.

mum's NECKLACE

I will get this back!

I told Horace and Jasper everything I'd heard and got them on board to help me get back Mum's necklace. Horace is happy I've finally found THE ANGLE, my reason for taking the job at Liberty in the first place. He never believed I was working just to fulfill my dreams and explore my passion, but I had. Now I'm not so sure. Maybe the whole reason for my meeting the Baroness was so I could pull off one of the most impressive jewel heists in history.

Horace, Jasper, and I have started planning. I go to work as normal, but instead of looking for ways to further my fashion career, I am preparing for the future crime scene. The deliciousness is in the details. Every day around the same time, the Baroness covers her eyes with cucumber slices and takes a nine-minute power nap. As soon as she's lying down, I tiptoe out of the room and explore Ipswich Manor. I've marked down every single security camera. I've figured out who the guards are, when they change shifts, and who has keys to what. I've made different escape routes for Horace and Jasper so no matter what happens, we'll be able to make a quick exit. WE COULDN'T BE MORE PREPARED.

While the Baroness power naps,
I scope out the manor.

This stylish look helps me keep up appearances while I scope out the manor.

Icon

Exterminator Ensemble

JEWELRY HEIST CHECKLIST

✿ Wink disguised as rat
✿ Disable the security system
✿ Bypass the cameras
✿ Lift the key off the head of security
✿ Estella tosses key to Horace
✿ Open the safe
✿ Steal the necklace

Lipstick = Lfc.

Wink makes the cutest little rat.

IPSWICH
MANOR

The plan is easy: I'll get the key for the safe and distract the Baroness and her guards. Horace will break into the safe while Jasper keeps watch. We'll get out as fast as we broke in.

There's only one pesky little problem. . . . I can't go to the ball as Estella. The Baroness would recognize me. I need an alter ego, an elevated disguise.

I went to this charming thrift store called SECOND TIME AROUND, where the owner, Artie, has fabulous taste. Every piece I found was more unique and interesting than the last. The vintage House of Baroness collection is especially useful for my purposes. . . .

INSIDE SECOND TIME AROUND

DRESS DESIGN IDEAS

- gown from the Baroness's 1965 collection
- cape for big reveal?
- cutouts at the neckline
- high collar
- full skirt or mermaid train?

Here's to . . . cruella.

Black and White Ball Design Part One

WHITE CAPE DESIGN

—glittering white fabric
rigged with flash paper
—keep hood up so hair is a
dramatic reveal

I must've checked my reflection in the mirror a dozen times before I left for the ball last night. I'd covered every inch of my fabulous RED DRESS with a glittering white cape rigged with flash paper. The black cane was a nice touch and would serve as an impromptu weapon if (more like when) I needed it. I made sure my new black-and-white hair was hidden under the hood. I wanted DRAMA. I wanted the element of surprise.

Everything went smoothly at first. Jasper and Horace posed as exterminators to gain access to the building where the ball was being held. Jasper went to the control room to disable the security system while Horace, with a disguised Wink, pretended to spray for rats, slowly making his way to the safe. And me? I strolled up to the Black and White Ball looking FABULOUS and then made my way into the center of the room, blending in with the rest of the crowd. I watched the Baroness from afar. She mingled with the guests, complimenting some on their outfits, ridiculing others. I waited until the moment was just right to pull the focus from her and onto me, WHERE IT BELONGED.

At one point she stood up in front of her guests to give a toast. I positioned myself so I was right next to a tower of sparkling flutes, all stacked on top of each other. "Here's to me . . ." the Baroness announced. Before she could fully raise her glass, I knocked my elbow into the tower, and the whole thing toppled over and CRASHED to the ground. The entire room turned and stared at me. That was when the fun really began. . . .

THE BARONESS'S BLACK AND WHITE LOOK

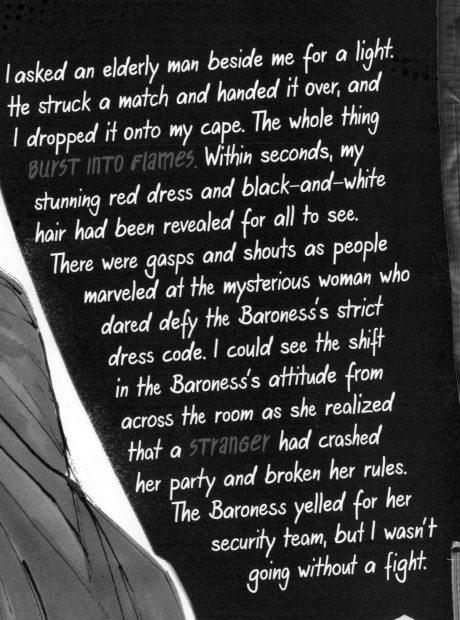

I asked an elderly man beside me for a light. He struck a match and handed it over, and I dropped it onto my cape. The whole thing BURST INTO FLAMES. Within seconds, my stunning red dress and black-and-white hair had been revealed for all to see. There were gasps and shouts as people marveled at the mysterious woman who dared defy the Baroness's strict dress code. I could see the shift in the Baroness's attitude from across the room as she realized that a STRANGER had crashed her party and broken her rules. The Baroness yelled for her security team, but I wasn't going without a fight.

Final dress features:
✿ layered fabric
✿ tulle underneath for body
✿ sweetheart neckline
✿ high collar
✿ red silk

Black and White Ball Design Part Two

One of her guards, a big HULKING brute, grabbed my arm. I screamed that he'd broken it, and he let me go. Then the Baroness's head of security ran over and tried to grab me, but I tripped him and he went down. I swiped the KEY TO THE SAFE from his jacket pocket and tossed it to Horace, who was waiting on an upper balcony. Just as Horace ran off to open the safe, six of the Baroness's guards surrounded me.

FACING DOWN THE GUARDS

"So obviously there's six of you, so you're going to win," I told them. "But the first two of you to arrive are going to be very badly hurt. So decide amongst yourselves who that is." The men looked around. One by one they rushed toward me. I struck the first two with my cane. But when I raised it again, that valet grabbed it, and I had nothing to defend myself with. He gripped my arm and dragged me toward the Baroness.

Mask Design:
❁ crow feathers
❁ glitter
❁ black tweed fabric

I did my best to keep my composure and channel Cruella as I was forced to speak with the Baroness. She said I looked familiar, and I told her I wasn't familiar—I WAS STUNNING. My name was Cruella and I had saved her horrid excuse for a dress from obscurity. As she asked if my hair was real, I worried she saw Estella under my dramatic look.

"Sit, I insist," she finally said. "I'm intrigued, and that never happens."

I didn't have a choice. The guards I hadn't maimed were surrounding us at that point. As I made my way to the chair, her three DALMATIANS growled in my direction.

The sight of them flanking her on both sides . . . it took my breath away. The memory of that night came back to me. I could still hear their horrible barking echoing in my ears. "Aren't they gorgeous?" the Baroness said. "And vicious. It's my favorite combination."

Baroness and guests at the Black and White Ball

I tried to make small talk with her, but it was hard to concentrate. I noticed she was wearing my mum's necklace; it wasn't in the safe like we expected. When I looked up, I saw Horace being marched across the balcony by the security team upstairs. He'd been APPREHENDED, and from the looks of it, he hadn't managed to get a single piece of jewelry.

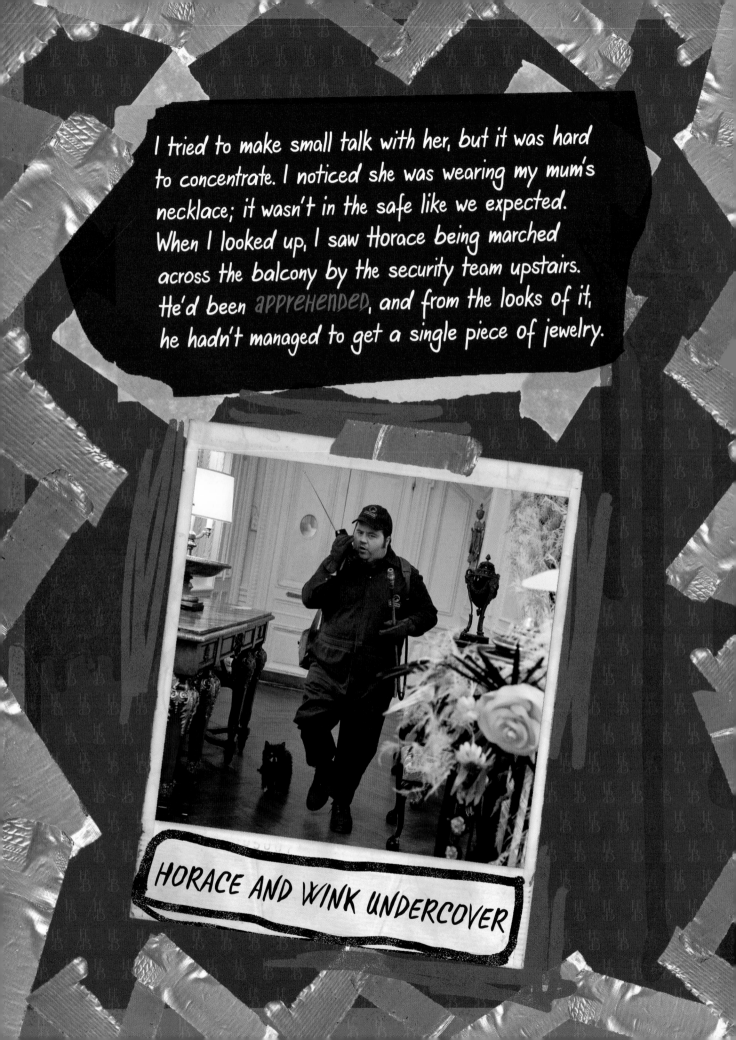

HORACE AND WINK UNDERCOVER

Nothing was going according to plan. I cursed to myself and then eyed the necklace, which sat at the Baroness's throat. I knew it was my LAST CHANCE. If I could just keep the Baroness talking, maybe we'd make off with at least one treasure.

"I want to be like you," I said. I went on, sometimes flattering her, other times saying meaningless drivel to keep her talking. A few minutes passed, and then I noticed Jasper emerging from the kitchen in a server's jacket, holding a covered silver tray. He must've seen me on the security footage and come out to help. He walked toward our table, ready to create a DISTRACTION so I could get away. I kept glancing down at my mum's necklace, and then I blabbered on, trying to keep the Baroness engaged so she wouldn't notice him.

But the Baroness was growing restless. She said she was done and was going to have me ARRESTED for trespassing. But then, just in time, Jasper strode up and set the silver tray down on the table in front of us. He lifted the lid with a flourish. Underneath were three plump, ugly rats.

JASPER TO THE RESCUE

A genius, that Jasper is.

The room broke into CHAOS. One rat jumped onto the Baroness's lap. She was panicking, really just losing it, and I took my chance to yank the necklace from her throat. I tossed it to Buddy, who'd been hiding under the party tables, and he ran off. I was smart and did the same. As I weaved through the crowd, guests screamed and pushed toward the exits. Horace took a flying leap off the balcony to escape the security team and landed on a giant cake below. The sprayer backpack I had designed for him went off and started shooting mist everywhere, shielding us from view. People were coughing and crying, unsure what it was. I kept running, pushing through the crowd, as Buddy darted toward another exit.

<u>THAT'S WHEN I HEARD IT.</u> The Baroness must've noticed the necklace in Buddy's mouth, because she screamed, "That dog! Stop! Thief!" and pulled a WHISTLE from her back pocket. She blew into it, and the sound split the air. I had to cover my ears, it was so deafening.

All at once, I was back on the lawn of Hellman Hall. I could picture my mum standing at the edge of the cliff. That sound I had heard, THE RINGING—it was the Baroness's whistle. In that moment I realized the Dalmatians hadn't crashed into Mum. THEY'D BEEN CALLED.

All the pieces started falling into place. Not only had the Baroness been the woman on the cliff that night with Mum, but she had also called her dogs to attack her, just like she called them to attack Buddy. My mum hadn't fallen from the cliff in a horrible accident . . .

. . . she had been murdered.

The rest of the night went by in a blur. Buddy made it to the exit, but one of those awful Dalmatians managed to get the necklace from him and SWALLOWED IT DOWN in one gulp. After Jasper pulled me out of the building, I had to hot-wire an old DEVILLE to get us all out of there. I pressed down hard on the accelerator, not caring how fast we were going. I just needed to get as far away as I could.

As I drove us back to our base, all I could think of was that high-pitched sound and the image of my mum falling backward, her eyes full of fear. For years, I'd relived that night over and over, questioning why I hadn't just listened to Mum when she'd told me to stay put. Why did I have to disobey her? What business did I have at that party? If I hadn't run out onto the lawn, those dogs never would've gone after her. I thought if it weren't for me, she would still be alive.

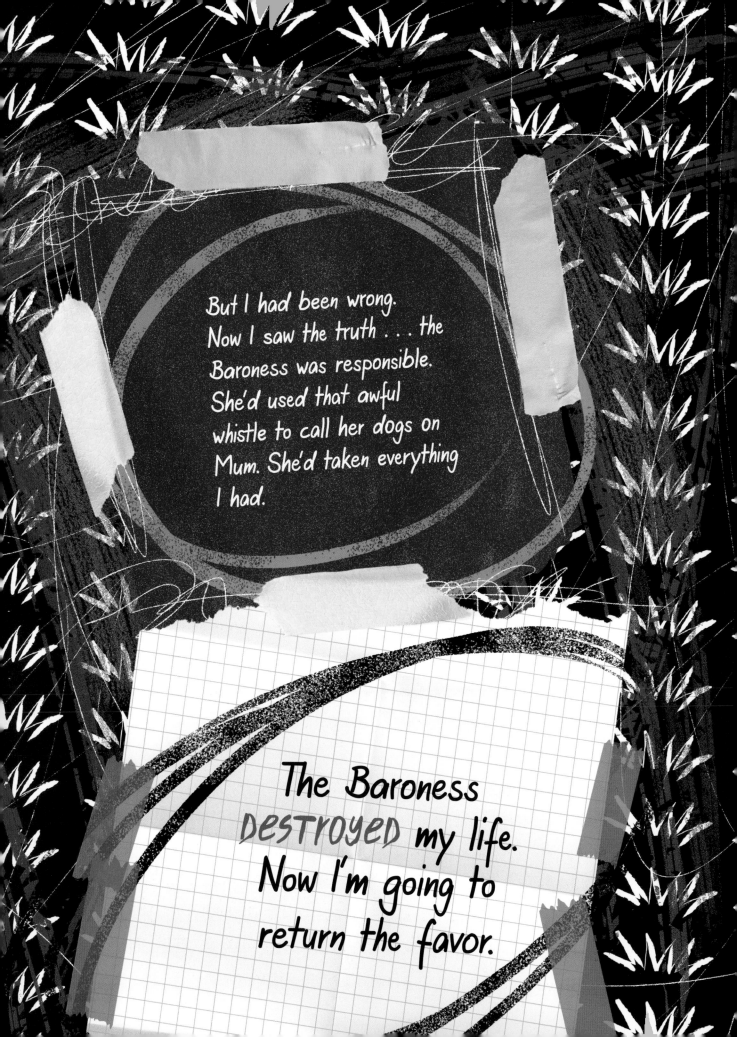

THE TATTLETALE

RATS ... AND A MYSTERY WOMAN!

BY ANITA DARLING

The Baroness's iconic Black and White Ball was in full swing last night when a mystery woman appeared and seemed determined to disrupt the event. The woman, who is still unnamed, proceeded to light her cape on fire, revealing a bright red gown underneath. The move stunned guests, many of whom have long been familiar with the Baroness's strict dress codes. The stunt seemed to be a deliberate attempt to ruin the monochrome revelry.

The Baroness has since reported the white-and-black-haired woman stole a valuable necklace, which at the time of publication is still missing. The theft was attempted just after a waiter unleashed a tray of rats in the dining room, creating a chaotic scene, with many guests trampling each other on their way to the exits. It is believed the mystery woman was working with two other men and two dogs, one of which is described as wearing a jaunty eye patch. All five fled the party in a stolen DeVille.

Sources close to the Baroness report her being "unnerved" and "threatened" by the mystery woman, who many believe is an aspiring fashion designer. The red gown has been identified as being from the Baroness's 1965 collection and was completely reinvented with an edgier, contemporary look. Only time will tell if the woman will make another spectacular appearance. This reporter, for one, certainly hopes so.

PANTHER DEVILLE

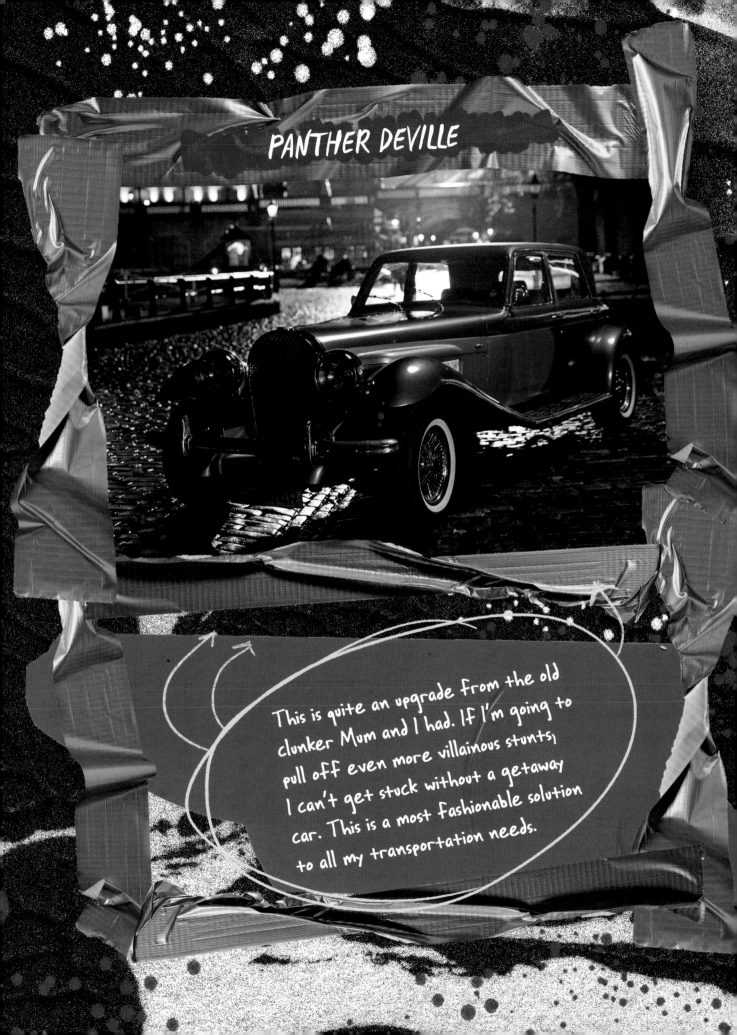

This is quite an upgrade from the old clunker Mum and I had. If I'm going to pull off even more villainous stunts, I can't get stuck without a getaway car. This is a most fashionable solution to all my transportation needs.

After the ball, I started to plot my next moves. Dear, polite Estella doesn't have the stomach for revenge. No, Mum's daughter would only think about forgiving and forgetting. That's why I let my *Cruella* side come out to play. Yes . . . Cruella will do what Estella can't.

TATTLETALE VISIT ENSEMBLE

STEP ONE of my new plan was to have Horace and Jasper steal the Baroness's Dalmatians and get the necklace back. But it wouldn't be enough to just take the necklace from the Baroness—no. I needed to steal what she cared most about in this world: her power. Her influence.

STEP TWO of the plan involved recruiting a couple of additional hands.

I put together this simple but stylish outfit for my next appearance as Cruella.

While Jasper and Horace went off to collect the Baroness's Dalmatians, I waited all morning in the TATTLETALE lobby, excited to see my old school friend. "Anita Darling, my darling!" I called out when she walked in. I thought I'd recognized Anita amongst the reporters at the Black and White Ball. There was something about her that had seemed familiar, but it wasn't until I saw her byline in <u>Tattletale</u> that I realized who she was. It turned out she had recognized me, too. She remembered all my wild days in school.

Anita hasn't changed a bit since we were kids. I am glad I can't say the same about myself. . . .

ANITA

"I'd like to start my own label," I said when we were finally done with the chitchat. "Why don't we work together to create some buzz for this old rag that you continually fill with this old hag?" I said, referencing the Baroness. Anita was intrigued by the idea. She'd gotten a lot of attention after reporting my stunt with the rats. That, and I think she'd always admired my extreme side. We agreed. It was time to introduce Cruella to the rest of the world.

ARTIE

After getting Anita to agree to my scheme, I walked into Second Time Around dressed in my Cruella best. Artie was reading about me in *Tattletale*. When he noticed me in his shop, I had to explain to him that I was the same young woman who'd come in just days before and bought the vintage evening gown. My stunt at the Black and White Ball as Cruella? That was just the beginning . . . but if I wanted to create my own fashion label, I'd need help beyond Horace and Jasper, who thought oversized burlap trousers were a perfectly acceptable way to dress. . . .

Artie's Fashion Staples
❀ bold print
❀ eyeliner
❀ a funky hat
❀ fun accessories

"I'm just getting started, darling," I told him. "And I need some help. I want to make art, Artie, and I want to make trouble. You in?" He looked at me with a smirk. "I do like trouble . . ." he said, tilting his head to one side. And just like that, we had our own two-person fashion label.

CRUELLA IN CHARGE

With Artie on board, we turned the lower level of the Lair into a design space, and I bought several dresses from Second Time Around to reinvent with my own flair. Here are some of the designs.

Perfect is overrated.

Red-and-white train completes the look.

Bold is beautiful.

Trousers with an extra-high waist

Can anyone lend me a hand?

While Artie helps sew my designs for my new fashion line, Horace and Jasper take care of the Baroness's stolen Dalmatians. Every day I go to work as Estella, the Baroness's sad, mousy assistant, and every night is Cruella's chance to shine.

When I overheard that the Baroness was going to a fancy premiere, I knew Cruella had to be there, too. I crashed the event in style on a moped. I wanted my entrance to scream: CRUELLA IS HERE TO STAY. I wanted it to turn heads and ruffle feathers.

FASHION
TERROR

MOPED STUNT LOOK

❁gold sequins on trousers
❁rubber from slashed tires
❁black face paint
❁gold helmet

Horace and Jasper have been grumbling about my being "bossy" and "mean" and ordering them around, which I do not appreciate. They don't like Cruella coming out to play.

But the truth is I needed their help to add a little extra flair to my next stunt, where we stole the paparazzi's attention from the Baroness during her most recent event appearance. I wish I could have seen the Baroness's face when the bottom of my gorgeous gown trapped her inside her car while outside all the tabloids clamored to get a photo of Cruella.

CAR STUNT LOOK

❁uniform jacket, decorated general

❁shoulder pads and gold tassels

❁Horace and Jasper to lock the doors in place (black straps to blend in with the limo)

❁detachable red-and-burgundy skirt, enough fabric to cover entire car

❁THE PAST scrawled across the skirt in pink and black paint

❁skirt must hide Baroness

THE TATTLETALE

ONE WOMAN'S TRASH IS ANOTHER WOMAN'S TREASURE BY ANITA DARLING

Last night Cruella stunned an unsuspecting crowd when she arrived at a red-carpet gala by garbage truck. The fashion designer and performance artist dumped a pile of vintage House of Baroness dresses onto the street, then emerged from the center in a regal evening gown with 40-foot train. Her latest stunt was one of her most impressive, requiring spotlights, staging, and several accomplices. A source close to the Baroness reveals her mounting anxiety over Cruella, who openly mocks the Baroness with each entrance. She's nervous about her new collection, the source says. She knows the pieces need to be better than a couture Cruella, otherwise her career is over. Done.

It Should be Fun!

People everywhere are wondering who Cruella is. Well, I am about to show them. . . .

GARBAGE STUNT LOOK

❀ fabric must be in stark contrast to the dresses dumped from truck
❀ rig spotlights; must pull truck onto correct mark
❀ BARONESS ENTERPRISES scrawled across side of truck
❀ 40-foot train to billow out behind me

The Baroness is coming undone, and I'm loving every minute of it. After my little stunt as Cruella at her red-carpet event, the Baroness has been screaming about how her new collection has to be her best collection. She even put her lawyer Roger on the task of finding out who this Cruella character is. I just sat there, creating new looks for her on my House of Baroness pad, trying to hide my smirk.

House of Baroness
LONDON

of Baroness
LONDON

House of Baroness
LONDON

Look at these dated designs the Baroness has me creating. Soon she will see what real fashion is.

It's so delicious watching the Baroness panic after each time Cruella upstages her. I'm taking away her power, her relevance: it's slipping away one glorious day at a time. And little does she know, while her assistant Estella continues creating boring designs for her next show, Cruella is busy whipping up outfits for a truly fabulous collection.

I have too many designs to count, but I've put some of my favorites here.

shoes ready for the runway

These outfits take all those bland beiges and grays the Baroness uses for her clothing and combines them with fierce pops of color. When people see my clothes, I want them to know that Cruella is the future.

Skirt or trousers?

mixed fabrics to create a textured look

I love mixing masculine and feminine styles together to create outfits that are truly unique. Here are some designs that use red, white, and black to make a statement.

red fabric acts as belt

House of Baroness
LONDON

Signature Dress

✿iridescent fabric
✿sweetheart neckline
✿mermaid gown with pleats
at the waist

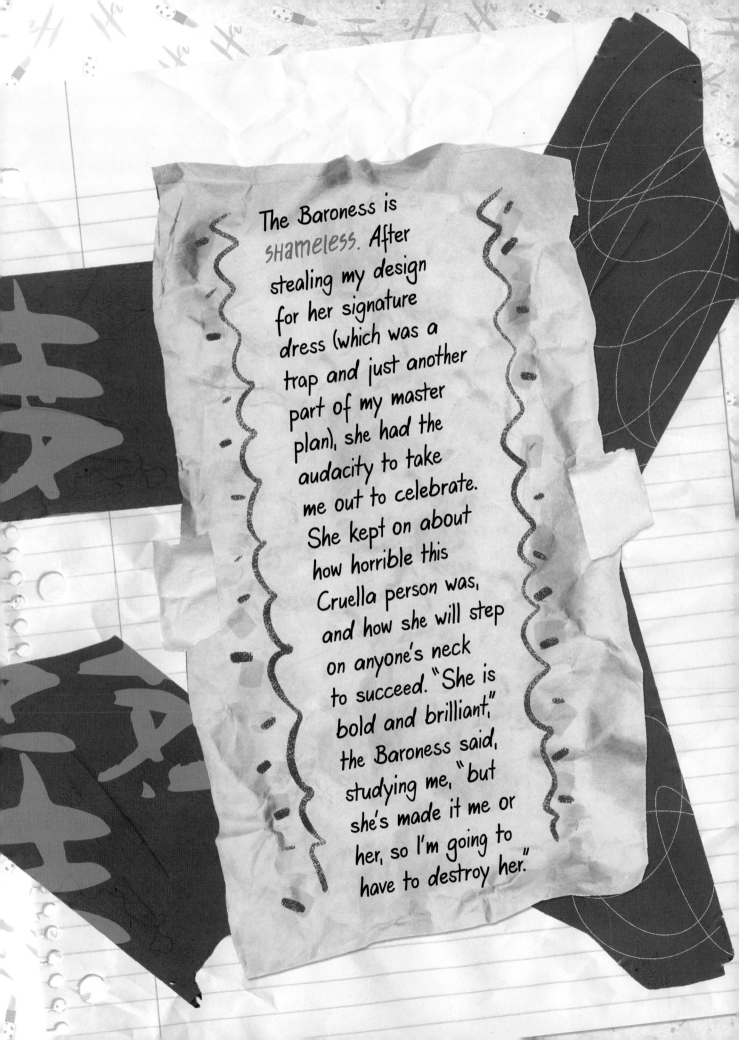

The Baroness is SHAMELESS. After stealing my design for her signature dress (which was a trap and just another part of my master plan), she had the audacity to take me out to celebrate. She kept on about how horrible this Cruella person was, and how she will step on anyone's neck to succeed. "She is bold and brilliant," the Baroness said, studying me, "but she's made it me or her, so I'm going to have to destroy her."

Sabotage Ideas

For the beading:
🌸 miniature stink bombs?
🌸 paintballs?
🌸 capsules filled with
petrol?

There was something about the way she looked at me. . . . I have the uneasy feeling she might suspect something. Is it possible she knows I'm Cruella? Has she recognized me?

Soon it won't matter. My plan is already in place, and she has taken the bait.

DINING WITH THE DEVIL

THE BARONESS'S DALMATIANS

Horace and Jasper are still waiting for one of the Baroness's PRECIOUS POOCHES to poop out the necklace. Wink and Buddy seem to really love them. (Horace, too.) It's eating away at the Baroness, the idea that she might never see her dogs again, but I've barely had any time to revel in her misery. I've been too busy executing the rest of my plan. In order for the signature dress I designed for the Baroness's collection to do its thing, it has to be in a closed space with the other gowns. I finally decided to create these STUNNING iridescent beads to hold moths' eggs. Once they hatch, it will be bye-bye to any fabric in their way. But I couldn't just tell the Baroness what to do, so I came up with a way to make her my puppet. . . .

Last night, Horace and Jasper staged a break-in at the Baroness's warehouse. It was a big, blustering attempt meant to be noticed and put the Baroness on edge. She had been trying to anticipate Cruella's next move, and this was the perfect thing to throw her off. Now she's worried Cruella is going to steal her entire collection.

night goggles to see in the dark

gloves to hide fingerprints

all black to blend in

WAREHOUSE BREAK-IN ENSEMBLE

It worked just as I'd planned. They wheeled in a giant safe and loaded all the gowns inside. Now those beautiful custom beads can do what they were always meant to. . . .

SETTING THE TRAP

Oh, if only I could have seen the Baroness's face when she opened the vault and discovered her precious collection in *ruins*. It must've been marvelous, the sight of those glittering moths as they flew out, leaving the tattered gowns in their wake.

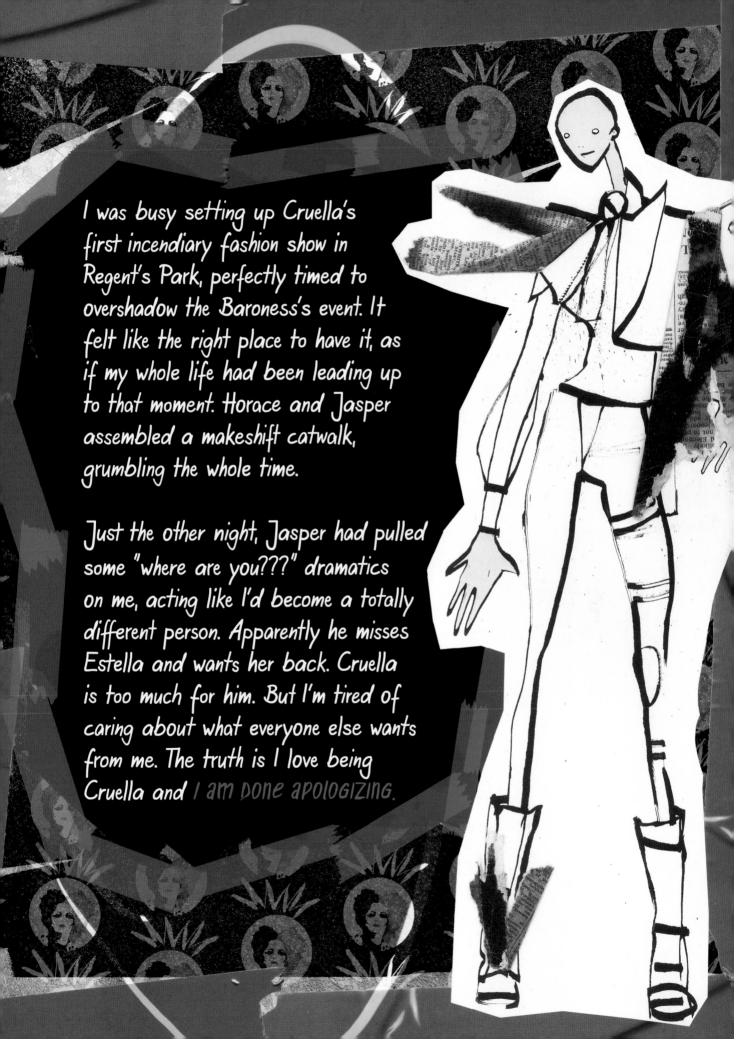

I was busy setting up Cruella's first incendiary fashion show in Regent's Park, perfectly timed to overshadow the Baroness's event. It felt like the right place to have it, as if my whole life had been leading up to that moment. Horace and Jasper assembled a makeshift catwalk, grumbling the whole time.

Just the other night, Jasper had pulled some "where are you???" dramatics on me, acting like I'd become a totally different person. Apparently he misses Estella and wants her back. Cruella is too much for him. But I'm tired of caring about what everyone else wants from me. The truth is I love being Cruella and *I am DONE APOLOGIZING.*

We used a bunch of models Artie knew from the London fashion scene for the show. I kept trying to forget about what Jasper had said. Instead I watched as they strode down the runway in different looks, each one more shocking than the last. Anita's stories had created a feverish buzz. The entire park was packed with people, all waiting for my appearance, some standing on benches to try to get a better view. The outfits were somehow bold and brilliant while at the same time colorful and restrained. Nothing had ever felt as good as being seen as the fashion designer—the artist—I'd always known I was. The true me.

Runway Themes

✿ Fashion rebellion
✿ ART FOR ALL
✿ Face off against the establishment
✿ Show them who you really are
✿ Image is EVERYTHING
✿ Break the rules

JASPER ON GUITAR AT THE SHOW

Here are some of the highlights from the show. I knew I wanted my fashion show to have the element of surprise. What if high fashion weren't something you needed an invitation to? What if art is everywhere and made for everyone?

I walked down the runway last. I wore this fabulous belted coat I designed with fake Dalmatian print for the sole purpose of horrifying the Baroness. There was an audible gasp as I reached the end of the catwalk.

I held up my fist in the air and shouted, "This is the future!" as loud as I could, my voice carrying over the music. As I stood there, with the crowd cheering for my designs—for me—I'd never felt more powerful in my entire life.

CRUELLA IS HERE TO STAY

Runway Finale

✿faux fur neckline
✿thick black belt to
  cinch the waist
✿asymmetrical collar
✿play with black-
  and-white theme
✿color blocking

THE INSIDE SCOOP

FASHION RIOT IN REGENT'S PARK

BY HENRI RUTHERFORD

In the biggest scandal since Yves Saint Laurent was declared dead, the Baroness Von Hellman has canceled her show after a swarm of moths ate her entire collection. Maybe the moths knew something, because the House of Baroness is looking positively old and musty next to tonight's explosion of new couture icon Cruella, in what can only be described as a fashion riot in Regent's Park. A newcomer to the fashion world, Cruella has proved herself as a rebel, a provocateur, and a creative genius. Her aggressive, inflammatory style had Londoners jammed around the park's fountain, desperate to get a glimpse of her new designs. There was an audible gasp from the audience as she emerged wearing a Dalmatian fur coat, as the Baroness's beloved pooches are still missing.

THE FADING STAR

CRUELLA: DESIGNER OR VANDAL? BY LEEZA FLOYD

Last night, Londoners were stunned by a pop-up punk rock fashion show in Regent's Park. Cruella, the young designer responsible, has been criticized by many who believe she's nothing more than a cocky provocateur trying to create a name for herself in a competitive industry. Still others see her as a performance artist and innovative designer whose alternative looks laugh in the face of safe, traditional designers like Baroness Von Hellman. Opinions aside, the police are now seeking to question her about the crowded event, for which she did not have permits. There is also much controversy surrounding a Dalmatian fur coat she allegedly wore, which has animal rights activists calling for her arrest. Only time will tell if this Cruella is a true designer, building a brand based on talent, or a vandal who will ultimately meet her demise.

SO MUCH HAS HAPPENED SINCE THE SHOW.

The fashion riot was positively brilliant . . . at least until the police showed up. The crowd scattered and I didn't have time to regroup with Artie, Horace, and Jasper. Instead I walked home alone and picked up loads of Indian takeaway, thinking I'd bring it back to the boys as a surprise.

AND BOY, WAS I IN FOR A SURPRISE. . . . .

TAKING OVER

When I flipped on the light, I discovered Horace and Jasper were tied to two chairs and Wink and Buddy were locked in a crate. The Baroness and her bodyguards stood in the center of the Lair—my lair—looking pleased with themselves.

It didn't take a genuis to figure out the Baroness had learned my secret. I told her to let Horace and Jasper go. This was between me and her. "Oh, I will," the Baroness said. "They'll be going to prison . . . for your murder." For a second I wasn't quite sure what she meant, but then her bodyguards grabbed me and tied me to a chair.

I struggled against the ties as her lackies dumped petrol on the floor, but I couldn't get free. "I know you killed my mother," I called as the men dragged Horace and Jasper out the door, but the Baroness didn't so much as blink. "Goodbye, Cruella," she finally said as she tossed a lighter onto the floor. The FLAMES rose around me.

Soon the entire lair was an inferno. I couldn't see anything. The smoke was so intense it stung my eyes. I started coughing, and the last thing I remember was a shape coming toward me that resembled a man. Then everything went dark.

IT SEEMED LIKE THE END, BUT really IT WAS JUST THE START.

When I finally woke up, I was in a flat I'd never seen before. Buddy was licking my cheek, trying to bring me back. I opened my eyes and spotted Wink. They were both alive. We'd made it.

At first I didn't recognize the man sitting across from me. He looked so different out of his valet uniform. But he was the same man who'd chased me through Hellman Hall at the Baroness's party years earlier. He said his name was JOHN and he'd worked for the Baroness for decades. He'd pulled me from the fire and taken me to his flat to keep me safe. As I tried to understand what had happened, he handed me the gold necklace the Baroness's Dalmatian had swallowed. He explained he had found it in the ashes. He had recovered other things from the Lair as well, including this sketchbook. Then he told me the whole story, starting from the beginning.

The Baroness had never wanted children. She'd lied and cheated to marry the successful baron, and when she found out she was pregnant, she was FURIOUS. She had the baby, a daughter, born with distinctive black-and-white hair. When the Baron was away on business, she ordered John to dispose of the child. He would never do such a thing; he instead gave the child to the Baroness's maid, Catherine. My mum. She raised the child for years as though she were her own, loving her, encouraging her, and protecting her from the Baroness.

"You are her daughter," John said, but I still couldn't quite understand it. He unscrewed the locket on the necklace, revealing a small gold key. It opened a wooden box he kept on his mantel. Inside, there was a birth certificate—MY BIRTH CERTIFICATE. It proved everything he was saying was true.

At some point the Baron had changed his will to leave everything to his daughter. When the Baroness told him she had died, he believed her and was consumed by grief. He passed away soon after without changing his will back. Everyone thought his daughter was dead, so everything he owned went to the Baroness.

That means I'm the RIGHTFUL HEIR to his fortune. The mansion, the title . . . it's all supposed to be mine.

STILL TRYING TO PROCESS EVERYTHING, I LEFT.

A new plan was beginning to form in my head, but there was something I needed to do before I fully embraced my new legacy. Soon I was back at the fountain at Regent's Park. I wanted to talk to Mum the way I always had before. I told her that I finally understood. All those years she'd been trying to TAME me, to TURN me into someone less like the Baroness and more like the sweet, kind person she had been.

"I really tried to be that, because I love you," I said, tears stinging my eyes. "But the truth is I'm not sweet Estella, try as I might. I never was. I'm CRUELLA, born BRILLIANT, born BAD, and maybe a little MAD. That's me, and I'm not like her . . . I'M BETTER."

This is who I am, and this is what I have to do. I can't keep apologizing for being myself.

I TOLD MY MUM I LOVED HER ONE LAST TIME. NOW I WAS READY.

Home Fashion Daily

Exclusive look at Baroness Von Hellman as she prepares her estate for her upcoming Viking Gala.

HELLMAN HALL

Seeing this photo of Hellman Hall in the tabloids, I can't help but feel giddy. It was where I was born, and it's where I'm meant to be.

BEHIND BARS

I ended up stealing a GARBAGE TRUCK and breaking Horace and Jasper out of jail, where they were sitting in some dingy cell, framed for my murder. I know I've been hard on them, but I'd never been so relieved to see their grubby little faces. I just wish they'd been happier to see me. They were still quite angry about my calling them imbeciles, and ordering them around, and generally being rude and miserable company. They said they were finished with me. I have to admit, it stung just the tiniest bit. It doesn't exactly feel good when the people you care about the most decide you're RUBBISH.

I tried to explain what had happened. I told them about the Baroness and how she was actually my biological mother, and that's when they finally started listening to me. "As soon as the Baroness finds out I'm alive, she's going to come after me again. I have a plan, but I can't do it without you guys," I said. "I went a bit mad and I'm so sorry. You're my family."

It wasn't until I said it just like that that they stopped their whining. And I meant it, I did. They can be infuriating, but they're the only people in the world I can trust, and I wasn't going to let them get rid of me without a fight. Together we're going to stop the Baroness once and for all.

IT'S TIME TO RECLAIM WHAT'S MINE.

THE INSIDE SCOOP

CRUELLA DIES IN FIRE

BY GIGI CABERNET

A fire broke out in a flat belonging to the fashion designer Cruella. Sources close to the investigation report that Cruella and her accomplices had been squatting in the abandoned flat for many years. She was tied up by the two men before they doused the building in petrol and set it on fire. The men have both been arrested for the crime. Cruella is presumed dead.

The news has stunned the London art scene, which has come to look forward to the performance artist's elaborate stunts. Just recently, she held a "fashion rebellion" in Regent's Park, and many have been clamoring to buy looks from her new collection, wondering when it will go on sale. "She was a good friend," says a man named Artie, who asks that we not use his last name. "It's not fair. She was taken so soon. She was absolutely brilliant, and she had so much more to share with the world."

THE FADING STAR

BARONESS VON HELLMAN TO HOLD CHARITY GALA AT HELLMAN HALL

BY BEAU BAGATELLE

Baroness Von Hellman has announced her latest event, a charity gala at her rural estate—Hellman Hall. The event proves to be one of the hottest tickets in all of England. Lady McCobb, Sir Easton Halliday, and Jojo Starr are all rumored to have been invited.

A source close to the Baroness has said that guests have been asked to dress in accordance with a "Viking" theme, with tickets going for as much as ten thousand pounds.

The Baroness's charity gala is the perfect opportunity for us to strike one last time. Now I just need to let Anita and Artie know I am alive, and together we will take down the Baroness.

GALA LOOK

*black-and-white wigs
*all black fabric
*pointed shoulders

House of Baroness
LONDON

Dear Lady McCobb,

As you know, you've been invited to my annual charity gala at Hellman Hall. We ask that all guests follow a strict dress code. We've gladly provided a lovely ensemble for you. Please wear this with my compliments.

Best,
Baroness Von Hellman

DELIVERY SERVICE

TO DO

- ✻ steal client list
- ✻ sew outfits
- ✻ forge HB note cards
- ✻ deliver designs
- ✻ *GET revenge*

It was a glorious sight, dozens of Cruellas climbing out of their cars and striding into Hellman Hall for the Baroness's gala. They were all dressed exactly like me: black gowns and black-and-white wigs. The guards were FLABBERGASTED. They kept running around, trying to figure out who was the real Cruella. With John's help, Horace and Jasper locked all the Baroness's bodyguards in the library. Less than an hour into the party, the Baroness was completely unprotected.

ANITA CAPTURES THE CHAOS

I stood on a balcony in Hellman Hall, blending in with all the other Cruellas in the crowd and waiting for the perfect moment to set my plan in motion. . . . The Baroness was dressed as a warrior queen, still in the theme for the night, and she seemed positively rageful that her dress code had been undermined. She searched every face in the crowd, trying to find me. I snuck up behind her and lifted the DOG WHISTLE from her pocket. Then I slipped out a side door and went directly to the loo.

After a quick wardrobe change, I was back to ESTELLA. I stared at my reflection in the mirror. Estella had always been a little mousy, hadn't she? With her brassy red hair and glasses? It seemed laughable now that I might have continued through life like this, content to blend into the background. I was always destined for so much more.

I made my way across the lawn, to the same spot where Mum had stood years before. I took a deep breath, preparing myself for what would come next. Then I brought the dog whistle to my lips and let out one long, shrill call.

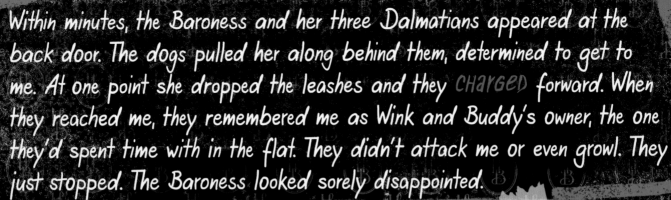

Within minutes, the Baroness and her three Dalmatians appeared at the back door. The dogs pulled her along behind them, determined to get to me. At one point she dropped the leashes and they CHARGED forward. When they reached me, they remembered me as Wink and Buddy's owner, the one they'd spent time with in the flat. They didn't attack me or even growl. They just stopped. The Baroness looked sorely disappointed.

"Hello, Cruella," she said as she came forward. "Hello, Mother," I replied. "I hate to ruin your party, but I came to evict you. This is my property." The Baroness laughed as I said it, her eyes widening in understanding. "It all makes sense now," she said, "that you're so extraordinary. Of course you're mine."

She seemed to notice that I paused, a little taken aback by her praise.

"Who else understands you?" she went on, not noticing that John was leading all the party guests onto the lawn, where they could see us. "Me. Your real mother. Who made a mistake and let something extraordinary go. I'm sorry."

It was hard to resist, the idea that she was proud of me—that she liked me just as I was, with all my BAD MOODS and MEAN THOUGHTS. No one had ever told me I was perfect just the way I was. I almost was ready to believe her. ALMOST.

But when she opened her arms to hug me and I stepped into them, I knew exactly what would come next.

"IDIOT," she whispered into my ear. Then she pushed me as hard as she could, and I fell backward, toward the ocean below, just as my mother had years earlier. I remember the camera flash as Anita took a picture. Then I was falling, the cliff farther and farther above me. I threw my arms up and there was a WHOOSH! as my cape filled, strengthened by the special corset boning I had sewn inside, catching the air underneath it. It acted as a parachute, slowing my fall. I gently touched down in the water. It wasn't long before Horace came by in a rowboat and pulled me out of the ocean.

I changed back into Cruella before joining the rest of the guests on the lawn. By that time the police were already there. They ARRESTED the Baroness for pushing me off the cliff. Everyone had seen what she'd done. They all assumed her dear assistant Estella was now dead, her body lost beneath the waves.

CRUELLA POST-GALA LOOK

It was so satisfying, watching that car haul her off to prison. The Baroness had never even considered that I might be **smarter**, more **cunning**, and **fiercer** than she was. She was so used to being number one that she didn't realize what I was capable of.

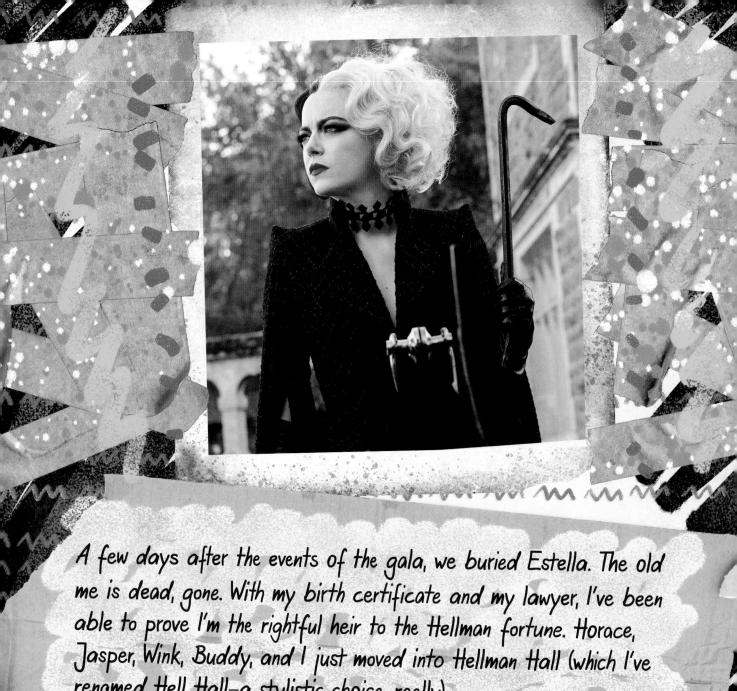

A few days after the events of the gala, we buried Estella. The old me is dead, gone. With my birth certificate and my lawyer, I've been able to prove I'm the rightful heir to the Hellman fortune. Horace, Jasper, Wink, Buddy, and I just moved into Hellman Hall (which I've renamed Hell Hall—a stylistic choice, really).

I'm writing this beside a cozy fire inside my new mansion. For the first time in a long time, life is truly good, and I'm having the strange anxious feeling that I need to get back to my fashion line, and to thinking up more devious plots. Everyone is too happy, too content. . . .

WHERE'S THE FUN IN THAT?